Slam Dunk Series

March Mania

Tess Eileen Kindig
Illustrated by Joe VanSeveren

CPH
SAINT LOUIS

To my son-in-law, Brian Watson, who introduced me to the delights of basketball (Go EMU!) and provides me with unending technical support.

Slam Dunk Series
Sixth Man Switch
Spider McGhee and the Hoopla
Zip, Zero, Zilch
Muggsy Makes an Assist
Gimme an "A"!
March Mania

Scripture quotations taken from the HOLY BIBLE, NEW INTERNATIONAL VERSION®. NIV®. Copyright © 1973, 1978, 1984 by International Bible Society. Used by permission of Zondervan Publishing House. All rights reserved.
Text copyright © 2000 Tess Eileen Kindig
Illustrations copyright © 2000 Concordia Publishing House
Published by Concordia Publishing House
3558 S. Jefferson Avenue, St. Louis, MO 63118-3968
Manufactured in the United States of America

Library of Congress Cataloging-in-Publication Data
Kindig, Tess Eileen
    March mania / Tess Eileen Kindig.
        p.cm. -- (Slam dunk series)
Summary: Mickey has trouble balancing the needs of his friends, his efforts to train his dog, school work, and practice for the upcoming championship game.
    ISBN 0-570-07092
[1.Basketball--Fiction. 2.Dogs--Fiction. 3.Friendship-- Fiction. 4.Christian life--Fiction.]
I Title.
    PZ7 .K5663 Mar 2000
    [Fic]--dc21   00-008210

1 2 3 4 5 6 7 8 9 10   09 08 07 06 05 04 03 02 01 00

Contents

Full Court Pressure!

"We did it!" shouted Tony and LaMar as they burst through the doors of the rec center. "We did it!"

My best friend Zack Zeno and I exchanged grins and took off at a run. If this was what we thought it was, our basketball team had just made the division play-offs.

"We're in?" I gasped when we reached them. "We're *really* going to play for the championship?"

LaMar nodded. "Yep. The roster's on the bulletin board. Coach is in the kitchen having coffee, but we saw it. First game's Saturday against the Wadsworth Wildcats."

Zack and I let out a groan. We'd lost to the Wildcats early in the season, the week I was benched for getting a technical. They're a mean team with a ball pass trick that reminds me of a game of "Hot Potato." It had our guys skittering around the floor like mice.

"Hey, don't worry about it," LaMar said, slapping me on the back. "We have you to help us out this time, Mick."

I grinned. "Yeah, that's right. The Eagles will grab those Wildcats by the scruff of their necks. All we have to do is sharpen our talons." I made imaginary clawing motions in the air and looked over at Tony.

Right away the grin slid off my face. The team would have me to help, but it wouldn't have Tony. He'd hurt his shoulder during an earlier game and then messed it up big-time at our fundraiser. We were unloading Christmas trees when he fell off the truck. The doctor said he can't play any more for the rest of the season.

"I wish you could be with us too," I told him. But even as I said it, I wasn't sure if it were true. In a way it was. I like Tony and it's fun playing with him. But if he hadn't gotten hurt I'd still be sixth man and Tony would be starting.

"Yeah, I'd like to be playing," Tony admitted. "But I'll be right there on the bench at every game. And next year I'll be back on the floor."

I gulped, already thinking about how hard it was going to be to defend my spot against him. But I'd worry about that later. The important thing now was getting ready to prove that the Pinecrest Flying Eagles were number one in the division.

The rec center buzzed with excited talk as we went inside. "You should see the trophy!" Luis Ramez cried. "It's huge, man! Must come clear up to here on me." He jabbed his waist with the side of his hand. "Won't it look great in the showcase?"

We all glanced over at the empty case lined with green felt. Already I could see the trophy in there, gold and shining. It would have the names of all the players on it—including mine, Mickey "Spider" McGhee.

The local newspaper nicknamed me Spider because they said it's like I have eight legs. I may be the shortest guy on the team and the shortest *person* in the entire fourth grade, but I'm so fast I'm a green and white *machine* on the court.

Behind us the door opened, bringing in a blast of cold air. Sam Sherman came through, blowing on his red fingers. He must have forgotten his real leather gloves today. "Hey, McGhee," he called, "there's somebody outside looking for you."

Sam's a starter just like Zack and me. But we aren't exactly friends. That's because ever since kindergarten his goal has been to make my life miserable. It used to bug me a lot. But that was before I found out that he's not as tough as he sounds. Oh, don't get me wrong. He can be mean as a snake and usually is. But underneath it all he's not so bad. It's sort of this weird secret we've shared ever since Valentine's Day two weeks ago.

"Who is it?" I asked.

"Your girlfriend." He batted his eyelashes and took on a high squeaky voice, "Oh, Mickey, you're so cuuuuuuuuuuute!"

He was talking about Trish Riley who is most definitely NOT my girlfriend. She's just a girl who lives down the street and is in my class at school. She's also a Pinecrest cheerleader. If it weren't for the monster crush she has on me, I wouldn't even mind her too much. It's just that I've decided not to get involved with girls until I'm at least 27. I figure I'm going to be too busy playing basketball before then. First in college and then in the NBA. I know my size is against me, but other short guys have made it big. Muggsy Bogues is only five foot three and he played for the Golden State Warriors. And Earl Boykins is only five foot five and he played for awhile with the Cleveland Cavaliers before signing with Orlando.

"What does she want?" I asked.

Sam shrugged. "How should I know? I'm not your messenger."

I ignored that and headed toward the door. "I'll be right back," I said to Zack.

Outside, Trish was standing near the flagpole jumping up and down to stay warm. "Mickey!"

she called when she saw me. "I've been looking all over for you!" The cheerleaders weren't supposed to be in the rec center while we were having practice. "I wanted to know when we're going to start Muggsy's dog training lessons. It's been two weeks since I gave you the certificate for free obedience school and we still haven't started our classes."

I shrugged. "I haven't had time, but we will," I promised. "Right now I have the play-offs to think about. I can't start anything new until after that." Trish had given me the lessons for Valentine's Day. Which was good because I can't afford real ones for my dog like she'd had for her own dog, Gabrielle.

"But, Mickey," she whined, tugging on the brim of her plaid baseball hat and giving me what I call her big-eyed, head-tilt smile. It's this dopey new grin she's come up with on account of the monster crush. It's supposed to be cute or something. "You said your mom is getting mad at Muggsy for chewing stuff up, didn't you?"

True. Just yesterday Muggsy jumped up on the table and made off with half a leftover pot roast. We found the bone on the floor of the linen closet. But I still didn't have time for any dog training lessons right now.

"Yeah," I agreed. "But I have to keep my math

grade up so I don't get benched right in the middle of play-offs. And Coach is really going to be working us. And March is when the college teams go to the NCAA. My dad and I will be watching a zillion games. There's a lot of pressure right now."

Trish tugged on her baseball cap and thought about that. "Well," she said finally. "I guess you aren't interested in the dog show then."

"Dog show?" In spite of myself I perked up. "What dog show?"

Trish knew she had me. She flashed me a 100-watt smile and stuck a piece of bright orange paper in my hand. Across the top it said, "First Annual Citywide Dog Show." I read the next few lines and felt my chin drop. The grand prize was a whole year of free pet food. And the best part was the dogs didn't have to be fancy breeds. That's important because my dad always says that God made Muggsy on Friday with all the leftover pieces from a week's worth of other dogs.

"Wow! Cool!" I said, "But I don't know, Trish…"

"There's a big trophy for the winner," she added. "*Plus* the chance to show off your dog. Remember how you were afraid everybody would think Muggsy was a little shrimp? Well, here's your chance to prove he's not."

Now she *really* had me. When Zack and I found Muggsy, his dog, Piston, and Trish's dog, Gabrielle, in the church parking lot, Muggsy had been the runt of the litter. It makes me feel bad to admit this, but I almost didn't want him because of his size. It didn't have as much to do with Muggsy as it did with me though. I thought the guys would laugh if they saw a shrimp walking a shrimpy dog. But now Muggsy was getting big—almost as big as Piston.

"Okay," I agreed. "When do you want to start the lessons? How about tomorrow after school?"

Trish grinned. "Deal. I'll be over at your house as soon as I change out of my school clothes."

I ran back inside. The lobby was empty. I started to head back to the locker room when I realized that everybody but me was in the gym already. Tony and LaMar had been dressed for practice when we arrived. And now Zack and Sam had dressed too. And I hadn't. I was late and Coach Duffy was going to be ready to hang me out to dry.

My heart pounded as I ran into the locker room and threw on my practice clothes. I didn't even have an excuse. At least not one he'd like. I couldn't very well say I was outside talking to a cheerleader. My mind raced as I tried to think of a way to make the truth sound good.

The door to the locker room opened and Zack poked his head in. "There you are!" he cried. "You better hurry up. Coach is ready to have your head."

"I'm ready. I'm ready," I mumbled, following him to the gym.

As soon as we opened the door everyone stopped doing jumping jacks and looked at me.

"What month is coming up, McGhee?" Coach Duffy barked.

"March," I answered, feeling my face turn as red as a crayon. Did I mention that I'm a world-class blusher? Well, I am. You just have to say the word "red" and my face turns it.

"And what happens in March?" he demanded.

"The play-offs," I answered.

Coach Duffy crossed his arms and glared at me. "That's right. Which means that now is no time to be out in front of the building talking to girls! It's time to get cracking! If you guys want to win, you have to work. No pain, no gain. Give me six laps, McGhee!"

I ran around the outside of the gym while the rest of the team went back to doing jumping jacks. I had been looking forward to March—the play-offs, the college games, the excitement. Every basketball fan loves March. But now I wasn't so sure. The heat was on—and I was already sweating!

2

Dulcie and
the Garbage Guy

Okay, Mickey, we're going to begin with the basics," Trish announced. She had just shown up at my house for dog obedience lessons. And already she was using a bossy voice I wasn't sure I liked.

"Wait!" I cried, jerking on Muggsy's leash to keep him from tearing into the street.

"See?" Trish demanded, in an even more know-it-all tone. "That's exactly why these lessons are so important. 'Wait' isn't a real command. You're supposed to teach Muggsy to heel."

I sighed. I hadn't been talking to Muggsy. I'd been *trying* to talk to Trish. I tried again.

"I meant for *you* to wait," I told her. "I don't want to do this heel thing until we can get Muggsy to stop chewing on stuff. The chewing is the biggest problem. It's making my mom nuts."

Trish tugged on her Cleveland Browns cap. "Well," she informed me, "it just so happens that I did a little research on that and I know what the problem is. Muggsy is teething."

"Teething!" I yelped. "You gotta be kidding. That's what babies do. Muggsy! Knock it off!"

Muggsy had found a dead bird on the ground and was sniffing it like a piece of hamburger. I jerked him away and looked across the street. The door of the house across from mine burst open and a tiny torpedo shot out. It was my neighbor, Dulcie Steffins. She's only four, but she thinks she's as old as we are. Not long ago, Zack and I babysat for her while her parents moved into their house. You wouldn't believe the stuff that happened.

The most important thing you need to know about Dulcie, though, is that she only has two speeds—fast and faster. And two volumes—loud and louder.

Well, maybe there's one more thing you need to know. She has an opinion about everything and isn't afraid to tell it to you. Oh, and she also has the wildest, fuzziest hair that ever grew out of a human head.

"HI, MICKEY!" Dulcie screeched, racing to the curb. "I'M COMING OVER! CROSS ME, OKAY?"

"No way," Trish began, "This is a serious lesson and …"

"Okay!" I hollered to Dulcie. Anything beat

listening to Patricia Ann Riley, Dog Expert of the World.

I looked both ways for cars. When the coast was clear I called, "Dulcie Ann Steffins, come oooooon dowwwwwwwwwwwn!" just like the guy on "The Price Is Right" on TV.

Dulcie tore across the street to our side. "So, what are we doing today?" she demanded when she was safely on the curb.

It cracks me up the way she automatically thinks she's included in everything.

"*We* aren't doing anything," Trish snapped. "But *I* am giving Mickey and Muggsy a dog obedience lesson."

Dulcie grinned. "Good," she said to Trish. "I'll help." She crouched down on the ground and went nose-to-nose with Muggsy. "YOU DO WHAT WE TELL YOU TO, YOU BAD DOG!" she hollered.

I laughed. Trish jumped between Dulcie and Muggsy. "Don't you yell at that dog!" she yelled at Dulcie. "I'm the one in charge here. If you want to watch, you can stand over there." She pointed to the grass next to the street. "Got that?"

Dulcie just shrugged. "Okay," she agreed. "Whatever." Whatever is Dulcie's new favorite word. I don't know where she learned it, but lately she's been sprinkling it into her speech like sugar on a Christmas cookie.

"Okay, now listen," Trish said to me in that same annoying boss-of-the-world voice. "Let's get back to what I was saying about teething. Muggsy is losing his milk teeth and getting his…"

"Oh, that is soooooooooooo dumb!" Dulcie interrupted. "Anybody knows that teeth can't be made of milk! Teeth are hard and milk doesn't get hard unless it's ice cream."

Trish ignored her. "He's losing his milk teeth and getting his grown-up ones and his gums hurt, so …"

Dulcie sank to her knees and pried open Muggsy's mouth. She tapped on his teeth with her fingernail. "See? This dog's teeth aren't frozen," she informed Trish. "They're hot. They're very, very hot dog teeth."

Trish swiped both hands down the side of her face and groaned. "How am I supposed to do this with her here?" she demanded.

She was talking to me of course. Like I had an answer. All I knew was that so far we hadn't done one thing to help Muggsy. He was jumping up on Dulcie and dancing on his back feet like a hyper ballerina.

Trish glared at Dulcie. "One more peep out of you, Dulcie Steffins, and I'm taking you home," she warned.

She turned back to me. "Okay now, Mickey.

Here's my idea. I think what's happening is that Muggsy needs something to chew on. And since you aren't home most of the time, he chews on anything he wants to. His gums hurt, he's bored and he ..."

Dulcie crossed her arms and let out a huge sigh. My feelings exactly.

"Uh, Trish," I cut in. "This is taking kind of long. Couldn't you maybe—uh—just teach me something that will make him stop?" I hated to sound ungrateful. These were free lessons after all. Not to mention a Valentine's Day present. But I had stuff to do. Like math. And practicing my hook shot. And about a zillion other things I could name.

Trish tugged on her hat and glared at me like *I* was the one needing the obedience lessons. "If you'd wait a second, Mickey, I'll tell you my idea," she snapped. "What I was *trying* to say is that you're gone all the time and Muggsy misses you. So he just chews on whatever he wants. We need to make him a video."

Now she had me. "A video? What kind of video? Where would we ever get a camera?" Questions tumbled out of my mouth like dice from a plastic cup.

Dulcie started to say something, then decided she'd better not. I could tell by her sparkling eyes that she loved the idea of a video though.

"A video of you," Trish said to me. "One that loops around and keeps playing. You can talk, play basketball, do whatever you want. Just so Muggsy can see and hear you all day. We have a video camera at home. I'll see if my mom will let us use it."

"Cool! When would we do it?" I figured I could play some jazzy music and do tricks with the ball like the Harlem Globetrotters.

"Saturday. After the game," Trish answered. She pointed to Dulcie. "But *she* stays home."

Dulcie's eyes blazed. "NO FAIR!" she hollered. "Tell her it's not fair, Mickey!"

Before I could answer, she whirled around and waved four fingers under Trish's nose. "That's a very BAD thing to do to somebody who's only this many, young lady," she told her.

"Okay, that's it! I've had it!" Trish snarled. She grabbed Dulcie's shoulder and turned her towards home.

Just as they stepped off the curb, a gust of wind grabbed hold of Trish's Cleveland Browns cap and spun it down the street like an autumn leaf. Trish screamed. Muggsy barked and lunged after it, dragging me behind him. I had no choice but to run. Zig. Zag. Across the neighbor's lawn we raced. Then back to my yard. Then to the neighbor on the other side's yard.

"Muggsy! Wait! Stop!" I yelled as we careened around a garbage can. My arm hit the can's metal lid on the way past, sending it flying like a frisbee. There was no time to pick it up. Muggsy was going to get that hat if he had to chase it to Siberia.

The hat teased the ground. Muggsy's paw shot out to grab it, but the hat took off again. Muggsy and I stormed back around the side of the neighbor's house. The hat landed on an empty paper towel tube sticking out of the garbage can. Muggsy jumped up after it. The can tipped and hit the ground with a crash.

"AARRGH! YUCK! PEWEY!" I screamed. The world's worst smell sent me staggering backwards.

Think dead fish. Sour milk. Rotten eggs. Slimy brown vegetables. All mixed together. I jerked on Muggsy's leash to slow him down. But he had the hat in his teeth and was raring to go. He jerked me forward—hard.

"Mickey, look out!" Trish screamed.

Too late. My foot wedged itself inside an empty coffee can and down I fell—face-first into the pile of stinky garbage. Muggsy strained at the leash. Trish grabbed him and held on as I yanked the coffee can off my foot. The front of my jacket was covered with broken eggshells. Slimy stuff dripped off my chin.

"Oh, yuck! Oh, yuck! Oh, yuck!" I screamed trying to wriggle out of my jacket. My hands fumbled with the zipper.

Inside the house I could hear somebody turning the lock on the basement door. I knew it was our neighbor, Mr. Keenan. I also knew what he was going to say.

He said it. Loudly.

"I'm sorry, Mr. Keenan," I said struggling to my feet. "It was an accident. We'll clean it up." I tried to wipe my face with the arm of my jacket.

"Well, you'd better," Mr. Keenan snapped. The door closed with a bang.

"Aren't you guys going to help?" I asked Trish and Dulcie. They just stood there staring at me.

Trish took a lady-like sniff and made a face. "I only agreed to do dog training," she said. "And anyway it's all *her* fault." She jabbed her thumb at Dulcie. "If she hadn't come barging over here, none of this would have happened."

"Don't you blame ME!" Dulcie screeched. "It's not MY fault! I'm only this many!"

I reached down and picked up a pork chop bone. They weren't going to help. They were going to fight. And Mr. Keenan was going to unlock the door and tell them to pipe down. He always says that—pipe down. It means be quiet, but it always makes me think of underneath the kitchen sink.

I picked up an empty yogurt container and tried to think of something that smells good. Peppermint. Flowers. Chocolate. Pizza. On second thought, forget pizza. What had once been pizza was lying on the ground growing green stuff.

3

Get the Lead Out, Zack

After the garbage accident I was sure I was going to come down with a terrible disease. I even got out my mom's fat red medical book and looked it up. According to the book, raw eggs carry something called salmonella. It sounds like the name of a pink girl fish, but it isn't. Salmonella is a kind of bacteria that will send your stomach whirling faster than a milkshake in a blender.

All night I waited to get it. But all I got were orders to take my jacket down the basement and wash it.

In hot water.

Now.

Which I did. But the next day on the bus I still got a whiff of garbage smell. It was the start of a very bad week. We began a new unit in math—the hardest one yet. Muggsy chewed my shoelace so Tuesday I had to go to school with my left sneaker flapping open. And Zack moped around all of Friday because Shawna Fox, this girl he likes, told Trish he has Dumbo ears.

Zack is living with my family until April while his dad works in Minnesota. He doesn't have a mom, so he either had to come to our house, or go live with an aunt and uncle he doesn't know in Chicago.

Most of the time I'm glad he chose our house. But this week hasn't been easy. Especially since he's off his game. I told him ten million times he'd better snap out of it. If we blow our chance against the Wildcats, we're out of the play-offs and done for the season.

"Why do we have to play the Wildcats first?" he complained the day of the game. We were standing at the edge of the court watching them lob balls. "This is too much pressure our first time out."

"Oh, come on, Zack! We can do it," I said. "*You* can do it. Just pay attention. Get in the game."

Zack grabbed a ball and tossed me a dirty look. "What do you think I've *been* doing?" he demanded.

I wanted to say "moping around," but just then the ref blew the whistle. Sam Sherman and a Wildcat moved to center court for the jump. The ref tossed the ball into the air and the Wildcat grabbed it and passed. His teammate jumped, caught it with an open palm, and passed it on. It was the usual Wildcat "Hot Potato" trick. Only this time we were ready for it. Quick as a silverfish, I darted in for the steal and snagged it. The crowd went wild. It was a big crowd too because we were the only team from our town to make it all the way to the finals.

"Spi-DER! Spi-DER!" they roared.

I looked around wildly. There were Wildcats to the right of me. Wildcats to the left. Wildcats in front. For half a second I panicked as I tried to weigh my odds. Could I make it to the basket?

Yes.

No.

Yes!

Too late. The Wildcats stole the ball and raced for their basket.

"Outta my way, Shrimpo!" Sam Sherman hissed, pounding past me. His arm slammed into my shoulder.

I staggered backwards trying to catch my breath as the Eagles stampeded by me. I knew I had to do something. *Anything*. A different Wildcat had the ball. He was dribbling, getting ready to go for the lay-up. I spotted an opening and shot through until I was right beside him. Both of us jumped at the exact same second. He let go of the ball and I strrrrrre-e-e-e-e-e-tched.

No good. The ball sailed through the hoop. I

was too short to knock it off its path.

"Dumb! Dumb! Dumb!" Sam Sherman growled near my left ear.

He was right. It *was* dumb. I should have known better than to pull a stunt like that. By halftime we were down six points and Coach's face was redder than the siren on an ambulance. The second we hit the locker room he was all over me.

"You're killing us out there, McGhee!" he barked. "Keep it up and I'm replacing you. Clemmons, be ready—you might be going in."

Anger tied a Boy Scout knot in my throat. What was Coach Duffy yelling at *me* for? Okay, so maybe I wasn't exactly tearing up the court, but at least I was trying. Which is more than could be said for Zack. All he'd done was run whichever way everybody else was running. It was like he had lead in his feet. But did you see anybody yelling at *him*? No way! Well, I'd show them!

I charged back onto court like a mad bull. Almost right away I got the ball. A Wildcat the size of a giraffe on stilts leaped in front of me. Squeak! Squeak! His fast-moving feet rubbed the wood like fingernails across a chalkboard as he worked to hold me back. I looked over at Zack. If only he'd get the lead out of his legs, we could pull off our best play. We'd practiced it a zillion times. But he didn't—or wouldn't—catch my eye.

I felt squeezed—until I saw LaMar nod. No way could I risk losing even a half second more. While the ball was still in the air, I zipped up to the basket praying that LaMar knew what to do. He caught the pass and sent it straight into my hands.

"Spi-DER! Spi-DER!"

The rumble of the crowd pushed me forward. I aimed. Jumped. Let go. Yessssssssssssss! The sound of stamping feet shook the bleachers. It was my basket. And I'd done it without Zack.

We won 41-38. But after the game Coach only pointed out what we did wrong. I thought he might at least tell me I did well with that one play, but he didn't. He acted as if I were invisible.

"What's wrong with you?" Zack asked while we were getting dressed. "You mad at me, or what?"

I shrugged. You bet I was mad. There was no room in basketball for laziness. And Zack hadn't pulled his weight. Everybody expected me to be perfect. But Zack could do whatever he wanted.

"I did the best I could, you know," he said when I didn't answer. It was like he could read my mind.

"Nice shot, Mick!" LaMar said, coming over to slap me a high five. "We work great together."

I slapped it back and grinned. "We sure do," I

said, still ignoring Zack. "We ought to do some one-on-one this week. Work out the kinks, you know?"

Zack didn't say anything and neither did I. All I wanted was to get home and see if Mom would make me a bacon, lettuce, and tomato sandwich. I grabbed my gym bag and left.

"Mickey!" a voice behind me in the hall shouted.

Trish. Today was the day we were supposed to make the video for Muggsy. With everything that had gone wrong, I'd sort of forgotten about it.

"Hey, Trish!" I replied, turning around. I stopped and waited for her to catch up. I could almost see her brain-popping ideas.

"Guess what? I have a surprise about our video!" she squealed, jumping a little on her toes. Her pompons rattled, a reminder of the game I'd rather forget.

I frowned. "What kind of surprise?" I wasn't exactly in a surprise sort of mood.

Trish's face lit up. "I can't tell you! If I told you it wouldn't be a surprise anymore. All I'm going to say is this—be at my house on time and don't bring Muggsy."

"Huh?" I wasn't sure I'd heard right. Why would we make a video for Muggsy and not even let him be in it?

"You heard me," Trish said in her bossy, obedience school voice. "Just do what I tell you to. It's a *very* good surprise. You'll like it."

I didn't want to get too excited about it. It was probably just some girlie thing only Trish and her friends would care about. But the way she said "very" perked me up.

"Okay," I agreed like it was no big deal. "Whatever you say. It's your video camera."

I hurried out to the car, still thinking about the video. I don't know why, but all of a sudden I wasn't even that mad at Zack anymore. Nobody can be on their game all the time. And we did win after all.

"Sorry I acted like a jerk at the game," I told him when we got to my room to dump our gym bags. "I was just afraid we were going to lose."

Zack shrugged. "Don't worry about it," he said. "It's all this pressure we're under. Is it just me, or do you feel like everything's speeded up all of a sudden?"

I flopped down on my bed and sighed. "Yeah, it's crazy all right," I agreed. "And now Trish tells me she's got some kind of surprise about the video. What do you suppose that's about?"

Zack opened the hamper and dumped in his dirty uniform. The hamper was so full he had to push the clothes down hard with his fist to make room. "Why do you even want to make that dumb thing?" he asked, ignoring my question. "You don't have time. Why don't you call her and tell her you'll do it some other day? The Akron Zips are playing at 2:00. It's going to be on TV."

I thought about that. It would be fun to stay home and watch the University of Akron game with Zack and my dad. We'd scream and pound on the coffee table whenever the Zips scored. Mom would make popcorn and hot cocoa with marshmallows. Maybe she'd even watch and yell right along with us. I like it when she does that. Especially when she gets mixed up and yells for the wrong team.

"Mickey! Zack! Lunch!" Mom called from the bottom of the steps.

The idea of staying home sailed out of my mind. "I can't," I said to Zack. "Muggsy needs this video. Come on, let's go eat. I smell bacon."

I gobbled down two sandwiches and a handful of Oreos and headed up the street. I hadn't gone far when a white van caught my eye. It was parked in Trish's driveway. My eyes popped. On the side in brown letters it said:

Saturday Night Video Productions
Professional Videos with Pizazz

4

Mickey in the Middle

"Wh-what's that about?" I asked Trish, pointing at the van.

She gave me the big-eyed, head-tilt smile and squeezed her hands together under her chin. "That's the surprise, silly! Isn't it great?"

I looked at the van again, then back at her. "I guess so," I muttered. "But I don't get it. We can't afford to hire somebody to make a video for a *dog*."

Trish pushed the screen door open wider and motioned for me to come in. "Of course we can't," she agreed. "That's why this is so great. My mom has a friend who makes professional videos. She told him what we were doing and he thought it might be an idea he could sell. He wants to use your video to get other people to make videos for *their* dogs. Cool, huh?"

"Yeah, cool," I said in a dazed voice. I was standing inside the front door. In the living room to my right I could see a man moving furniture and setting up lights.

"I told him you were very cute," Trish whispered. She grabbed my arm and yanked me into the bright light. "Ken, this is Mickey," she said to the video man. "The star of your video."

The word "star" curved my mouth into a smile. I smiled so hard my face hurt. You'd have thought I'd landed on a Hollywood sound stage instead of in the middle of Trish Riley's dinky living room.

"Hey there, Mickey," the man named Ken greeted me. "It's good to meet you. I guess Trish told you about our project. Stand over here under this light for me, will you? I want to see how you look on camera."

I shrugged out of my jacket and did what he said. The glare of the lights made me blink. I stared at the camera, unsure of where to look. "What should I do?" I asked. Already I could feel my face getting red—and not from the heat of the lights either.

"Do whatever you want," Ken answered. "But don't just stand there. Talk to me."

All of a sudden I felt like a class-A jerk. What could I talk about? I glanced over at Trish. She made some sort of wild hand motions at me, but I couldn't figure them out.

"Uh," I said, shuffling my feet. "My name is Mickey McGhee and I'm—uh—a basketball player." I stopped and looked around, then back at the camera. "This would be a whole lot better if I had my basketball," I said.

"Don't you worry about it. This is just a test. Forget the basketball, or just pretend you have it," Ken advised.

I fake-dribbled and grinned at the camera. I still felt pretty stupid, but Ken seemed happy. "Good! Good!" he said. "You're going to do just fine. You can stop now."

I walked out of the light and over to Trish. She was taping poster paper to the big sliding door between the living room and dining room.

"What's that for?" I asked, pointing at it.

"Our storyboard," she said in her obedience school voice. "Ken says you can't make a video until you have a storyboard."

I started to say that we weren't taping a story. It was just me, and maybe later Muggsy, messing around. But the doorbell rang before I could. Mrs. Riley came out of the kitchen to answer it.

"HI! I CAME TO MAKE THE VIDEO," a loud familiar voice announced from the porch.

"I hope that's okay," a grown-up voice added. "Dulcie told me she was supposed to come. She promised me that Mickey and Trish know all about it."

Trish grabbed both of her ponytails and yanked them out sideways. "Grrrrrrrrrrr! It's Dulcie," she growled. "Didn't I say she couldn't come?"

"Don't blame *me*," I replied, looking over at the door. "I didn't invite her."

Dulcie said good-bye to her mother and took off her jacket. As soon as she saw me she grinned and bounded into the living room. "I'M HERE!" she announced loudly, like nobody could see that. "WHEN DO WE START?"

"Well, aren't you cute!" Ken said, smiling at her. He focused the camera on Dulcie's face and crouched down to look at her through the view finder. "We could use some more talent."

Dulcie grinned. "That's GOOD!" she replied. "Because I have LOTS of talent. Do you want to hear me sing?"

"NO!" Trish and I roared at the exact same second. Listening to Dulcie sing is worse than having a bullhorn blown in your ear.

Dulcie glared at us. "I can dance like a football girl too," she told Ken.

Ken laughed like that was cuter than baby pictures. "Well, this isn't exactly a musical," he told her. "But you never know when we might work some of that in. The first thing we have to do though is think of things dogs like." He reached into his shirt pocket and pulled out a felt tip pen.

"Bones!" Trish hollered.

Ken shook his head. "Well, yeah. But I was

thinking of things that move. Things we could put in the video. Interesting things. Like maybe another dog."

"I have another dog," Dulcie offered. "Taco. He looks like the Taco Bell dog."

Ken wrote Taco's name down on the poster paper on the door.

"How about cats?" I asked. "Dogs don't usually like cats, at least not at first. But they think they're interesting."

"Good!" Ken said. He wrote down cats. "Who do you know who has a cat we could borrow?"

Ours isn't a very catty neighborhood. We couldn't think of a single person. But Trish's mother knew somebody from the school where she works who would let us film her Siamese.

By the time we finished brainstorming—that's what Ken called coming up with a list of interesting things—we had ten ideas. We settled on three for the video: Taco, the Siamese cat, and Muggsy and me acting like the Harlem Globetrotters.

"Okay, that's it for today," Ken said when we figured out what to include. "Let's meet again tomorrow and film the part with Taco."

"Wait a minute!" Trish protested. "What about Gabrielle? My dog is every bit as nice as hers and she's also bigger. AND she's Muggsy's sister."

Dulcie screwed up her face. "NO WAY, JOSÉ!"

she hollered. "I said Taco first. And the man said okay. He even wrote it down." She stomped over to the paper on the door and pointed to Taco's name.

Trish stuck out her lip. "Ken," she whined. "I really want to use Gabrielle."

I struggled into my jacket and ignored them both. It seemed like all anybody did anymore was fight. Well, they could just go at it. I was out of there.

Back home the game was almost over. I watched the Zips lose and went into the kitchen to see what was for dinner. Mom was making a salad. I flipped the switch for the oven light and looked inside. Some sort of chicken thing swam in a sea of tomato sauce.

"So, how's the video coming?" Mom asked as she tore lettuce into bite-sized pieces.

"Okay," I mumbled.

Mom popped a piece of lettuce into her mouth. "That's good," she answered when she'd swallowed. "I don't mind you making it, Mickey. But I hope you won't let it interfere with school. You're barely out of the woods with math. Remember?"

How could I forget? It was less than a month ago that I'd almost gotten an F. If Sam Sherman hadn't agreed to tutor me, I'd be sitting on the bench right now. During *play-offs*.

"I know," I muttered. "I'm fine. Don't worry."

Actually, I wasn't fine at all. We were studying graphs and I couldn't read a graph any better than I could read Chinese. I needed to study, but there wasn't time. There wasn't time for anything anymore.

"By the way," Mom said, whacking the head off a fat carrot. "I hope you haven't forgotten that you agreed to help me with the Sunday school lesson. I need you to make 25 paper basketballs."

I stared at the bubbling red sauce in the oven again. Somehow those basketballs had bounced right out of my brain. Mom had asked me days ago to make them and I kept saying I'd get on it. But I never did. I was so busy I'd even sort of forgotten about God. Not entirely, of course. I still said "Hi" in the morning and "Goodnight" before I went to sleep. But I wasn't exactly peppering heaven with prayers these days.

When I didn't answer, Mom said, "The trouble with being too busy, is that it's easy to forget the things that really count." She glanced at the clock. "Set the table for me will you, honey?"

I opened the kitchen cupboard and took out a stack of plates. Part of me knew Mom was right. But another part felt picked on. Why couldn't people see how much pressure I was under right now? How much did they expect a kid to do? It's not like I'm perfect or anything. And I wasn't ignoring God *completely*. Could I help it if all the stuff in my life was important at the same time?

After dinner I headed for the basement to make the basketballs for Mom's Sunday school class. I used an empty soda can from the recycling bin to trace the circle. Just as I was ready to start drawing the lines on them, the phone rang.

"Mickey! It's for you!" my little sister, Meggie, hollered down the steps. Whenever a phone rings you can count on her to answer. It doesn't matter where she is in the house. Before anybody has a chance to even think about picking it up, she's already got it.

"Who is it?" I hollered. Saturday night was a weird time to be getting a phone call. Especially at 9:00. Meggie didn't answer. I threw down my brown marker and trudged up to the kitchen.

"It's Trish," Meggie whispered. "And she sounds really mad."

I sighed and picked up the phone. "Hey there, Trish," I said into it. "What's up?"

"I'll tell you what's up, Mickey McGhee," she snapped. "*I'm* up! And I should be in bed getting my beauty sleep …"

I let that one go.

"But I can't because that neighbor of yours and

her yappy little dog are making me crazy. Ken is my mother's friend and I think I deserve to have Gabrielle be in the video. After all, if it weren't for me there wouldn't even *be* a video."

"I know that," I said in a reasonable voice. "But what do you expect me to do?"

"Get rid of Dulcie," Trish snapped. "Or forget the whole thing."

5

Juiced Up

I didn't *want* to forget the whole thing. Muggsy needed a video. And I needed—okay, make that *wanted*—to be a star. If Trish didn't want Dulcie to help us, why didn't she just tell her so herself? Why did I have to be the bad guy? It was so unfair. I was about to pop. I had so much pressure and now she hands me this! But did I say any of that to Trish? No way.

"Okay, I'll see what I can do," I muttered.

I caved. I know it. And I was mad at myself for it too. I'm not always such a wimp, but I just didn't want to get into a big argument when I still had all those basketballs to make.

I started to go back down the basement, but headed to my room instead. I didn't even turn on the light. I just flopped down on my bed in the dark and stared at the band of light the streetlamp was making across the ceiling. I needed to pray. I knew it. I even wanted to do it, but it seemed pretty cheesy to be asking God for help when I'd checked out for two weeks. I asked anyway.

And He heard me, I know He did. It's just that He didn't have fast answers in mind. I lay there for awhile, then went back down the basement and finished the basketballs. A few of them looked more like brown eggs than basketballs, but I let it go. Cutting has never been my best thing, but tonight I couldn't seem to keep my eye on the lines. Mom frowned when she saw the messy ones, but she didn't say anything.

"Mickeeeeeeeey! Phooooooooone!" Meggie hollered up the stairs the next day when we got home from church. Zack and I were in my room changing out of our good clothes.

I hopped into some jeans and headed for the kitchen. Already I was dreading the sound of Trish Riley's whiny voice.

"MICKEY, I NEED YOU! RIGHT NOW!" an excited voice that wasn't Trish's bellowed in my ear. "A BAD THING HAPPENED. YOU HAVE TO HELP ME!" Before I could answer I was listening to a dial tone.

Mom was at the stove stirring tomato soup. "Is something wrong, Mickey?" she asked.

"That was Dulcie," I said, hanging up. "She sounded pretty freaked out. She said something bad happened. She wants me to come right over. Do you mind if I go?"

Mom waved toward the kitchen door. "Go

ahead," she said. "I'll just put your lunch in the fridge."

I grabbed my jacket and ran around to the front of the house. As soon as she saw me, Dulcie started screeching again.

"HELP ME, MICKEY! HELP ME!!!!" she screamed, waving a cordless phone in one hand and Taco's leash in the other. Both she and her skinny, hairless dog looked like they were doing a Mexican Hat Dance.

"What's the matter?" I called as I ran across the street.

I didn't need an answer. Even before I reached the porch I knew. Dulcie and/or Taco had had a run-in with a skunk. The smell burned my nose and flooded my eyes with tears. "Oh, man!" I cried, taking three giant steps back. I coughed and wiped my arm across my watery eyes. "Where did you find a skunk?"

"I *didn't* find any skunk," Dulcie said. "Taco did. He had to go outside early this morning, so my mom took him. He ran under the porch. And then there was this big noise and he came out smelling ker-pewy.

"What should I do, Mickey? My dad went to Cindernatty and my mom says Taco can't come in the house. And Trish won't let him in her house either. And now he won't be able to be in the video." Her chin quivered. Any second she was going to burst into tears.

I looked at Taco, then at my watch. I had half an hour to get over to Trish's. Suddenly I had a thought. The skunk might just be the answer to my prayers. Especially since Dulcie's dad was in Cincinnati and not able to help.

"Gosh, Dulcie," I said in my most understanding voice. "I think you're probably right about the video. It takes a long time to get rid of skunk smell. Maybe some other time."

"DON'T YOU TELL ME THAT!" Dulcie screamed, cutting me off. She stamped her foot and glared at me. "BE A GOOD NEIGHBOR AND HELP ME AND TACO!"

I sighed. I didn't have a clue how to help. But maybe my mom did. She works part time for the Humane Society. "Okay, okay," I told her. "Stay put and I'll go find out what to do."

Dulcie glared at the "stay put" part, but did what she was told. I sighed again as I headed back across the street. There wasn't a chance I was going to be able to get Taco smelling good in half an hour. Already I could see my video landing on the trash heap.

"Tomato juice," Mom said firmly, when she heard about the skunk. "Taco needs a bath in tomato juice. Let me call Linda."

Linda is Mrs. Steffins, Dulcie's mother. Mom picked up the phone and dialed her number. When she answered, Mom told her about the tomato juice remedy. "Don't worry," Mom assured her when she finished. "Mickey will take care of it. And he'll do anything and everything he can to make sure Taco gets to be in the video."

Oh yeah? "Anything" and "everything" were at least fifty jillion times more things than I was willing to give. Of course I didn't want to hurt Dulcie's feelings. But I had a video to make. Why couldn't people get it through their heads that I was BUSY?

"Mrs. Steffins only has tomato paste," Mom said after she hung up. "You can use that too, but go down the basement and get a big can of juice from the fruit cellar."

The fruit cellar doesn't have anything to do with fruit. It's just this little room in the basement with shelves where Mom keeps canned food. I pulled the chain on the light and quickly found what I was looking for. It was a huge can—as big as maybe five regular-sized cans put together.

The thought of sticking Taco into a big bowl of bright red juice cheered me up. If we added a little hamburger, cheese, and a tortilla, he really would be a taco!

That's when it hit me. The skunk *was* the

answer to my prayers—just not the way I'd thought at first. I raced up the steps, grabbed the phone, and dialed Trish's number.

"Hurry! Get down to Dulcie's with Ken!" I shouted when she answered. "And bring the camera. We've got ourselves some real action here!" Before she could protest, I hung up and ran across the street to Dulcie's with the giant can of tomato juice under my arm.

Mrs. Steffins gave us a plastic dishpan for the juice. Then she took the can inside the house and brought it back opened. "I wish I could help," she said with a wad of tissues over her nose and mouth. "But the smell is making me sick. Are you all right, Dulcie?"

"I'm GOOD, GOOD, GOOD!" Dulcie squealed. "Mickey made Taco be in the video anyway."

At least I hoped that's what I'd done. Ken's van pulled into the driveway just as Dulcie and I were pouring the juice into the dishpan. He and Trish hopped out and headed up the walk.

"What's going on?" Ken called.

Trish bent over double in a coughing fit. "Oh, gross! Skunk!" she sputtered when she could finally talk. "This is even worse than garbage! How could you bring us down here for something so disgusting, Mickey McGhee?"

"Wait!" Ken cried. He turned away from the porch, took a deep breath of fresh air and turned back. "This could be good. Jump in there, Trish. All of you give the dog a bath and I'll tape. Just act normal."

Dulcie picked up the squirmy Taco and set him in the pan of tomato juice. His skinny legs churned the red juice, splashing it right in my eye.

"Owwwwwwwwww!" I howled, letting go of my grip on his chest. Dulcie stuck both hands into the juice up to her elbows. The sleeves of her pink jacket turned an ugly red. She was no match for Taco though. He hopped over the side of the pan and bolted down the steps.

"TACO! TACO! COME BACK!" Dulcie cried running after him. Drops of tomato juice from her dripping arms sprayed all over Trish.

Trish let out a scream that would make Tarzan jealous.

Ken zoomed in on Trish's howling face, then took off at a run after Dulcie and Taco. I stood on the porch rubbing my stinging eye as they ran around a tree and into the backyard. No way was I chasing any tomato-flavored dog. I had had enough dog chasing this week to last a lifetime.

"Look at my jacket!" Trish wailed. "It's all red! And it's my cheerleading jacket too!"

All the cheerleaders had green and white jackets that said Pinecrest Cheerleader on the back. I knew how much Trish liked hers, so I felt sort of bad for her.

"I bet your mom can get it out," I said in what I thought was a comforting voice. "And if she can't, you could maybe get a bunch of pins and cover up the stains."

Trish grabbed her ponytails and let out a howl. "You just don't understand anything, Mickey McGhee!" she screamed. "This is all your fault. I told you I didn't want Dulcie to be part of this video!"

Before I could defend myself, Dulcie and Ken came around the side of the house. Taco dangled from Dulcie's arms like a purse. His little pink tongue hung out of the side of his mouth. He looked like he'd just run the Boston Marathon.

"We got him!" Dulcie announced as if we couldn't see that. She plopped the dog back into the juice. This time he stood there and howled.

The sound was pretty funny coming from such a little mutt, but Trish didn't laugh. She crossed her arms over her chest and glared at Dulcie and me. I knew better than to ask if she wanted to help with the bath. Ken zoomed in for a close-up as Dulcie held the dog and I washed the top of his head. When we were done, Dulcie lifted him out.

"Get that dog away from me!" Trish screamed.

She jumped out of the way just in time. Taco shook like a tree in a windstorm, sending a shower of tomato juice flying.

"This is great!" Ken cried, moving in for an angle shot. "We couldn't have staged something this good."

Dulcie and I wrapped Taco in an old towel and rubbed him down. When we took the towel off, we burst out laughing. Trish stuck out her lip and pouted.

Taco was as pink as a cloud of cotton candy.

6

Picky, Picky!

"No way!" Zack cried. "The dog's really pink?"

"Pink as a petunia," I answered, grinning.

We were up in my room coloring our natural resource maps of the United States for social studies. If you didn't count Florida, mine looked good enough to hang up for the Open House.

Zack laughed. "That's funny! Only don't you think you're wasting a lot of time, Mick? When's the dog show?"

The dog show! Somehow the video had wiped the dog show right out of my brain. "I don't know. Next week?" I asked uncertainly.

Zack shoved back the chair from my desk and stood up. "See this?" he asked, picking up the wastebasket in the corner.

I peered inside at a confetti of yellow, gold, blue, green, pink, and white paper.

"That USED to be the money from my Monopoly game," Zack informed me. "Muggsy had himself a little party this afternoon. I hate to say it, Mick, but there's no way that dog's going to be ready to be in a dog show in only a week."

I sighed and put the cap back on my red marker. It's true that we'd spent a bunch of time on the video. Time that had been taken away from Muggsy's obedience school lessons. But it would be worth it. Once the video was finished, Muggsy would stop exercising his gums on our stuff. And—if I got lucky—I might even become a video star. It would really help out my basketball career.

"He'll be ready," I said to Zack. "Just wait. He'll be *ready*."

Zack shrugged and sat back down. "Whatever you say, Mick," he answered. But it was clear he didn't believe it.

Deep down I wasn't sure I believed it either. How was I ever going to study math, practice basketball, watch games, compete in the championship, make a video, AND teach Muggsy how to walk on a leash without wrapping me up like a mummy—all at the same time? I was only one person. One extremely busy, misunderstood person.

The next day I cornered Trish at school. "I guess we need to take some time to work on that heel thing with Muggsy after all," I told her. "The dog show's next week."

Trish tugged on the brim of her baseball cap.

That was a good sign. She always tugs on the brim of her hat whenever she talks to me. Only this time the big-eyed, head-tilt smile was nowhere in sight. *That* was a bad sign.

"I'm not teaching you anything, Mickey McGhee," she snarled.

"Huh?" I was confused. "But you have to! You gave me a certificate that said the lessons were good for life!"

Trish shook her head so hard her ponytails whipped around faster than Muggsy's tail. "Too bad," she said glaring. "Because I'm taking them back!"

"That's not fair!" I protested. I could feel my face getting hot. "You said you'd help. What did I ever do to you?"

Trish glared harder. "You know what you did!" she stormed. "You chose Dulcie and Taco over me and Gabrielle. Since that's your choice I think you ought to let Dulcie help with the obedience lessons."

My mouth dropped open as she stomped off to join her friend Brittany by the swings. Trish was actually jealous of a four-year-old and a skinny, hairless dog! I shook my head. It didn't seem possible. It was too stupid. But it was true. And now I was on my own with one more thing to do.

I trudged over to the door where Mrs. Clay was

telling a bunch of first graders not to climb up the front of the slide.

"Mrs. Clay, can I go to the library instead of recess?" I asked. "I need to look up something."

Mrs. Clay looked at me like I'd just said I wanted to learn to speak Japanese. You can't blame her I suppose. I like to read, but for me recess means playing basketball. Unless there's too much snow. Then I stand around with the guys and talk about basketball.

"Of course you may go to the library," she said, writing out a hall pass for me from the handy pad she kept on a clipboard. "But don't be late getting back to class. We're having a speaker."

I thanked her and hurried inside. In the library I grabbed every book I could find about dogs and speed-read through them. Each writer had a little different idea about training, but the one I liked best involved using a clicker. The idea was to click and give the dog treats every time he responded to your command. Then when he got so used to responding, you didn't have to click or reward him anymore. I couldn't wait to get started.

But it wouldn't be tonight. I had basketball practice and I knew Coach would work us until we dropped.

As soon as I walked into the rec center I could feel the tension. The team seemed stiff and grouchy. And sparks flew off Coach every time he moved. The second we got out on the floor he shrilled his whistle until his cheeks looked like they were storing oranges.

"Last week was the pits!" he barked. "You guys won by the skin of your teeth. All I can say is, it must have been a miracle."

The team shifted uncomfortably. I sneaked a peek at Zack out of the corner of my eye, but he was staring at the floor. I knew he thought Coach was talking about him. But he was really talking about all of us.

"This week we face our final match—against the Seville Pirates," Coach continued. "And you all know what happened last time."

We shifted uncomfortably again, remembering how we'd lost. Never mind that I'd racked up an amazing three-pointer at the end. It went right over the head of Marcus Bennett, a Pirate so huge he looked like he belonged in middle school. That didn't count. I hadn't been perfect. WE hadn't been perfect. Nowadays it seems everybody expected everything to be perfect.

My stress level cranked up a couple of notches as I imagined a second meeting with the towering Marcus Bennett. This time in the play-offs. In the final game.

"Okay, here's what we're going to do," Coach

said. "We're going to focus on screening. I'm going to show you guys how to set a pick. And I want you to listen because this can save your neck when you're in trouble out there." He walked around us, doing a complete circle while he thought it over.

"Mickey and Zack, you're the most likely pair," he decided, grabbing us out of line.

"Zack, you're the biggest, so you're going to set the pick for Mickey to either take a shot or to receive a pass. He's little, but he's quick. And quickness is what we're banking on. Okay, here's what you do."

Coach spread his feet wide and bent his knees a little to form a good solid base. Then he clamped his right hand over his left wrist and held them down low. He looked like it would take a hurricane to knock him over.

Zack copied his position. It didn't look too convincing.

Coach turned to me. "Okay, Mickey. Your job is to set up the Pirates's defensive man. First you lead him a few steps away from the screen—then *whammo*! Just when he gets comfortable, you pull a fast one. You either run in the opposite direction or change your pace. Anything that will fool him. But you have to stay close to the pick. Even a foot between you will give him a chance to move into the space."

We practiced the play until sweat dripped off me like the tomato juice had dripped off Dulcie. Every single time Zack blew it. He failed to set up the screen until it was too late. I knew it should be me and LaMar doing this, but I couldn't say anything. Coach was in no mood for suggestions.

"Move to the right, Zeno!" Coach yelled after the fifth or sixth time. "No! Your OTHER right! Okay, forget it! That's it! All I can say is, you guys better pray for another miracle."

In the locker room I didn't say anything to Zack until everybody left. Then I grabbed my gym bag and muttered, "Hurry up! My mom's waiting." I knew I sounded snarly, but I didn't care. All Zack had to do was stand still. How hard could that be? I was the one who had to work.

Zack grabbed his bag and followed me to the front door. I shoved it open and stepped out into the cold. Mom hadn't shown up yet, but I needed the fresh air to cool me down—and not just from all the activity either. Zack followed me outside. I wished he hadn't. I really didn't want to talk about it.

"You're mad," he said flatly.

I shrugged. No way did I want to get into a fight. I was too tired and I had a math quiz to study for. Those graphs would take all the brain power I had left.

"Yes, you are," he insisted. "Look, Mick, I'm sorry I messed up. I really was doing my best. I'll try harder at the game. I promise."

I shrugged again. Without Zack's full attention, the play was no good. It was a two-man deal. No matter how hard I ran, or what fake-outs I did, I was dead if Zack didn't screen me. And he wasn't pulling his weight. And hadn't been ever since we made the championships. The bottom line was I couldn't count on him. It was as simple as that. And this was the make-it-or-break-it game. I'd just have to depend on LaMar. I sighed. One more thing I had to do!

"Yeah, yeah. Whatever." I mumbled.

Zack dropped his gym bag on the concrete like he was too tired to hang onto it. "Could you maybe cut me a little slack here, Mick?" he asked. "I'm doing the best I can. But it's a lot of pressure being in the championships, you know?"

"Pressure!" The word exploded out of my mouth. "What do *you* know about pressure? *I'm* the one who's under pressure. You think it's easy doing all the stuff I'm doing? You don't even have the dog show or the video to worry about."

"Those things were all your choices, Mick," Zack said evenly. "You don't have anybody to blame but yourself. And you can get out of them any time you want."

True. All true. But Zack wasn't like me. I had thought he was, but he wasn't. He didn't want things as badly as I wanted them. I wanted to be a star any way and every way I could be one. And I wanted Muggsy to be one too. If that was terrible, then I guessed I was guilty.

Mom pulled up at the curb and saved me from having to say anything. I climbed into the front seat and slammed the car door extra hard.

"You don't seem too happy," she said to me as she waited for Zack to climb in back. "Something wrong?"

"No," I lied. I was just too tired to talk about it. My bones were tired. My skin was tired. Even my hair was tired. I was so tired, the stick-up piece on the top of my head was practically lying down snoring.

"Well, that's good, because I need a big favor," Mom said. "I need you to play with Meggie tonight while I run down to the church. The co-op truck arrived and they're short of volunteers. Dad will be home, but he wants to work on the drip in the shower." She glanced over at me, a small grin playing around her lips. "Unless, of course, you want to help at the co-op yourself?"

It was supposed to be a joke. Mom knows that the co-op and I don't mix. Every time I show up there to bag groceries there's a major clean-up involved. I don't care if stuff is cheaper and fresher at the co-op. I still think people ought to buy food from grocery stores—not from the basement of churches where they have to pack it themselves.

"That's okay. I'll watch Meggie," I said with a loud sigh.

"Good!" Mom answered cheerfully. "And while you're at it, you can set the table for dinner."

7

Like Cats and Dogs

The green plastic clicker made a crisp, clean popping sound. "Good, Muggsy!" I cried. "Good boy!"

Only it wasn't good. Or at least not very good. Every time Muggsy even came close to sitting down I was supposed to click and give him a treat. The idea was for him to slowly learn how to sit down and stay down. But after 15 whole minutes of my Mickey McGhee Personal Dog Training, Muggsy's tail brushed the ground for maybe half a second before he was back up running around in circles.

"We're all out of treats," Dulcie announced, turning over the empty plastic bowl. "Now what, Mickey?"

I didn't know what. Muggsy had gobbled 20 treats. All the treats we had. And he still flunked sitting.

"Wait here. I'll see if my mom will give us some baloney," I said finally. I tugged Muggsy's leash and pulled him back to the house. No way was I going to risk Dulcie watching him until I got back. I was permanently out of the dog-chasing business.

"One slice," Mom said when I asked for the lunchmeat. "And *only* one. I need the rest for tomorrow. Cut it up into small pieces."

"Okay," I said grabbing the baloney package. I peeled off a slice and ran out the door with Muggsy yipping along beside me. Muggsy likes doggie treats, but baloney sends him into orbit.

Outside, I waved the slice of baloney at Dulcie. "We're back in business!" I announced, plopping it into the empty dog treat bowl. "Tear it up into little pieces, okay?"

"Okay," Dulcie agreed. She set the bowl on the porch step and sat down beside it while I went back to working with Muggsy.

"Sit, Muggsy! Sit!" I urged.

Muggsy ran around in a circle.

"Sit, Muggsy!" I said again.

Muggsy saw a dog across the street and lurched after it. I dragged him back.

"Sit, Muggsy!" I commanded. My voice was beginning to sound as bossy as Trish Riley's.

It took 12 more tries, but Muggsy finally sat. Sort of. His tail hit the sidewalk for a split second. I clicked the clicker and reached into the bowl behind me for a piece of baloney.

My hand touched plastic.

"Good, Muggsy! Good!" I said, groping around in the bowl. I was supposed to keep my eye on the dog.

"Where's the baloney?" I shouted at Dulcie. "Quick! Hand me a piece! Sit, Muggsy! Sit! This isn't working. I should have had the treat ready as soon as he sat."

Dulcie didn't say anything. I whirled around and stared at her. "WHERE'S THE BALONEY?" I shouted.

Dulcie's eyes widened. "Gone," she said in a tiny voice.

"What do you mean gone?"

"Gone," she said, louder this time. "I ate it. You were taking too long, Mickey, and I was hungry." She stood up and shoved four greasy little fingers in my face. "I'm only this many, Mister!"

I let out a howl so loud you could have heard it in Siberia. At the rate we were going Muggsy had a better chance of winning the Publisher's Clearinghouse Sweepstakes than of winning a whole year of free pet food. We were doomed. Dead. Pet show losers.

"You're going home," I said to Dulcie when I stopped howling. "Right now! There's no point trying to teach Muggsy without any treats. And that was the last slice I had."

I couldn't believe it. Dulcie got up and meekly followed me to the curb. "Don't be mad at me, Mickey," she said. "I didn't know you didn't have any more. I'm sorry."

"Yeah, yeah, whatever," I muttered. I'd had it with Dulcie. And excuses. And being "this many." But mostly I'd had it with trying so hard to do so many things at once.

After I delivered Dulcie to her mother, I took Muggsy into the house and wandered down to Trish's. Today was the day we were filming the part with the Siamese cat. As usual, Muggsy didn't get to be in the video. But this time neither did Dulcie. In fact, Dulcie didn't even know we were shooting it. It made me feel sort of guilty. But not too guilty since she just ate my one and only slice of baloney.

"Hi, Mickey!" Trish hollered as I came up the walk. She was talking to me again. "Hurry up! Ken is going to try to film Gabrielle with the cat. Isn't that great?"

Yeah. Great. Gabrielle got to have fun while poor Muggsy had to stay home locked in the basement so Mom could cook dinner in peace. How fair was that?

"Yeah, that's good," I said, stomping snow off my boots so I wouldn't track up the house. "But dogs and cats don't get along too well. We could wind up with a fight on our hands."

Trish opened the screen door for me. "Oh, it's not a problem," she said. "Gabrielle and Banana love each other already."

Banana? The cat's name was *Banana*? Who would name a poor defenseless cat Banana, for Pete's sake? Life was getting weirder by the minute.

I took off my jacket and went into the living room. Gabrielle was toasting herself over the warm air register. Banana, the Siamese cat, was curled up beside her giving her a bath. Her little pink cat tongue scrubbed Gabrielle's ear like a scratchy washcloth.

"See?" Trish announced. "Didn't I tell you they were friends?"

"Yeah," I agreed reluctantly. "But that's not exactly what I'd call an action shot."

Trish ignored me and walked over to the cat. "Hey there, Anna Banana," she said, dropping to her knees. "You ready to show Mickey what you can do?"

The cat stopped licking. Its chocolate-colored ears twitched. Every muscle in its skinny body tensed. Two blue eyes gazed at Trish expectantly. Trish crawled over to the sofa and pulled a flashlight out from under a cushion.

As soon as Banana saw the flashlight she

jumped to her feet and let out the most amazing sounds you've ever heard come out of a cat's throat. Forget meows! She sounded like a bird chirping.

"Watch this!" Trish cried. "Are you ready to shoot, Ken?"

"Ready!" Ken said.

Trish shined the flashlight so that a small circle of light fell on the green rug. Banana sprang up like a leopard and darted after it. Trish skimmed the light along the floor. Banana darted back and forth, trying to catch it.

"Now, watch this!" Trish cried.

She flicked her wrist and made the light move in a slow, lazy circle. Banana crouched low and followed it, trying to pounce. Trish made the light spin faster and faster. Ken moved in for a wide-angle shot just in time to capture the crazy cat whirling like an amusement park ride. I didn't want to laugh—I was in a bad mood after all—but I couldn't help it. I laughed like a hyena.

Trish grinned at me. "If you think that's funny, watch this!" She swung the beam of light over to the sliding door.

A bright circle of white light danced along the dark wood. Banana went bananas! She leaped to catch the light and landed on her back feet with her front paws scratching at the door. It was perfect—except for one thing. Her left leg pinned Gabrielle's ear to the floor.

Gabrielle had been lying on the heat register watching. When Banana's back leg landed on her ear, she jumped up to her feet and growled. The sound came from deep in her throat—low and rumbly.

Before Gabrielle could do anything, Banana whipped around and hissed at her. Then one brown-tipped paw shot out and swiped Gabrielle across the face. Gabrielle yelped as a thin ribbon of blood made a line down the center of her black nose.

"Sssssssssssss! Get out of here, you bad cat!" Trish hissed. "Look what you've done to my dog!" She sank to her knees and threw her arms around her struggling pet. "Oh, my poor, poor baby!" she moaned.

Her "poor, poor baby" looked mad enough to have the cat for dinner. Ken turned off the camera and took Banana out to the kitchen. If he hadn't, she would have been banana pudding in five seconds flat.

For awhile it looked like we were going to have to give up on the cat idea. But by the time I went home, the two animals had made up again. Ken shot some good scenes with the flashlight and also with Gabrielle and Banana tussling.

But I never got on camera once. It was The Patricia Ann Riley Show. Mickey McGhee didn't even get to do a commercial.

8

LaMar, Lazybones, and Me

I trudged up the stairs to the kitchen in an even worse mood than I'd been in when I'd left for Trish's. I'd wasted a whole hour on the stupid video and never got to be in front of the camera for five seconds. And now I had to try to figure out graphs for math.

I knew I should be practicing basketball too—the big game was Saturday—but there was just no time. Unless maybe I could call LaMar and see if he wanted to do some one-on-one tomorrow. With any luck, I could fit it in before we filmed the third section of the video.

"Hi, Mickey! Somebody called you and Zack," Meggie announced as soon as I walked into the kitchen. She was sitting at the table brushing olive oil on slices of bread. "I washed my hands," she informed me when she saw me glance at the bread.

"Who was it?" Right now germs were the least of my worries.

Meggie shrugged. "I don't know, but he had

some bad news." She held up a slice of bread. "See, Mickey, I covered it all. No white spots. Now I'm going to sprinkle the garlic on it."

My heart speeded up in my chest. "What kind of bad news?" I asked, ignoring the garlic bread.

Meggie wrinkled up her forehead. "I don't know. Something about an a-pen-dis-is."

She sounded out the last word carefully, but I didn't wait around trying to figure it out. I raced up the stairs and into my room. Zack was sitting at my desk coloring his graphs for math.

"What happened? What's the bad news?" I asked, out of breath.

"LaMar," Zack replied in a flat voice. "He has appendicitis. He's in the hospital."

"What? That can't be! I just saw him today." I felt numb. Without LaMar the team was in big trouble.

Zack ran his hands over his face and sighed. "It's true," he said sadly. "Coach called while you were gone. LaMar got sick after school and had to be rushed to the hospital. They're going to take his appendix out. He'll be okay. But of course he's out for Saturday's game. Coach is putting Nick Clemmons in. He's also calling an extra practice tomorrow."

I sat down on my bed, too dazed to speak. Without LaMar there wasn't a chance we'd win.

Nick was a good player, but nowhere near as good as LaMar. With Zack playing so badly right now, I'd been counting on LaMar to support me.

Zack pushed back his chair and stood up. "Looks to me like we're dead in the water," he said.

My thoughts exactly. Even the extra practice wouldn't bail us out of this one. An extra practice also meant I wouldn't be able to shoot the third part of the video—the *good* part where Muggsy and I finally got to fool around with the basketball. Trish would probably get Ken to do something else with her and Gabrielle. I went downstairs and called her.

"Oh, that's too bad about LaMar," she said when she heard the news. "I guess we won't win, huh?"

Just what I wanted to hear—positive thinking. Even if I felt that way myself, it bugged me to hear her say it.

"We can win," I said gruffly. "LaMar's good, but he's not exactly the whole team. Anyhow, the reason I'm calling is that Coach wants another practice. I can't make it tomorrow. Can we shoot another time?"

There was a short pause. Then Trish said, "I don't know, Mickey. Ken is a busy man. I'll have to find out and let you know. We may have to go with something else. Like shots of cars and trucks, or other dogs with their owners. I don't know."

My heart took another nosedive. I had been looking forward to the third part of the video like summer vacation. Ken had said he'd dub in the music to "Sweet Georgia Brown," the Harlem Globetrotter's theme song, while Muggsy and I did tricks with the ball. Or at least while I did tricks with the ball. Muggsy would probably just run around and bark a lot.

The next day at practice Coach had Zack and me practice setting a pick again.

"Zack, you're not even paying attention!" he barked. "You're too slow. You've got to keep your eyes open and be ready to make your move. Try it again!"

We tried it again. And again. And *again*. But it was no use. Zack was so far off his game it's a wonder he even found the court.

"What's the matter with you?" I demanded when we got to the locker room. "You're blowing it, man!"

Zack slammed his locker door but didn't answer. I knew I was pushing him, but I refused to let this game go down the tubes. We'd worked too hard all season. Even if we didn't win, at least we shouldn't go down looking like total losers.

"Zack, what have we been shooting for since

clear back in the summer?" I demanded, wedging myself between him and the slammed locker door. "This! A chance to win the play-offs. And now we've got that chance and you're not helping me here."

Zack's brown eyes blazed. "Helping *you*?" he squawked. "What do you mean, helping *you*? You aren't the only player on the team, Mick—even though you think you are. You're running around doing all this stuff like you're the only person in the world. You don't care about anybody else's feelings but your own. Busy! Busy! Busy! Hah! You don't even care that you kept Dulcie out of the video. Or that you won't let Trish tell you anything about dog training. Or that I happen to be really, really freaked out."

Out of the corner of my eye I could see Sam Sherman watching. He was probably getting a big fat kick out of Zack and me fighting. Well, let him watch! I was working so hard and nobody appreciated it. And I'd had enough! If I didn't say what was on my mind, I'd burst.

"You're right! I *have* been busy!" I shouted. "But at least I'm doing something instead of moping around. If you don't get the lead out, Zack, we're in big trouble." I shoved past him, grabbed my bag, and headed outside.

I knew I'd ignored what he'd said about Dulcie

and Trish and about his feeling freaked. But that's because I didn't know what to say. Part of it poked at my conscience like a sharp needle. But another part of me felt like he was trying to cover up for being such a lazybones.

Back home Zack and I only spoke to be polite. I'd say, "Pass the chow mein, please." And he'd just say, "Here." All through dinner I could feel Mom's eyes watching me, trying to figure out what was wrong. But I stared at my plate and ate my food in silence.

After dinner I went down to the basement and tried to work with Muggsy for awhile.

"Sit, Muggsy! Sit!" I said.

Muggsy wandered away to examine the leftover Christmas wrap. He grabbed the end of a spool of skinny ribbon and took off running. By the time I caught him, he'd wrapped it around two poles.

I gave up and asked if I could go outside and shoot some hoops in the dark. It's the coolest thing. I turn on the light over the side door and it's like there's no one in the whole world except me and my basketball.

"Absolutely not!" Mom said. "You need to work on your math. I'm getting worried about that grade again, Mickey." She ran hot water in the sink and squirted in some dish soap.

She had plenty of reason to worry. Somehow, as

hard as I tried, there never seemed to be time for math. But *I* had plenty to worry about too. We had the biggest game of the season coming up. With Zack being down for the count and LaMar sick, I needed to be in top shape. "I'll do it later," I promised. "Please, Mom. Just let me go out for half an hour. Then I'll ..."

"No!" Mom snapped, surprising me. It wasn't like her to yell unless I was really driving her crazy. I guess I must have been driving her crazier than I'd thought.

"You march right up those steps and get at that homework!" she ordered, sliding the plates into the hot water. "I'm coming up to check on you when I finish here. If you're having problems, ask Dad for help."

That was it. No basketball practice for me. I made my way upstairs and went into my room. Zack was sitting at my desk, which meant I'd have to work on the floor or the bed. I grabbed my math book and sat on the rug with my back against my bunk.

Nobody said anything. I rifled the pages of the book. Graphs, pie charts, numbers, and geometry figures flashed by in a blur. I went back to the part with the bar graphs.

The first problem was:

Fifteen kids say pizza is their favorite food. Twelve vote for hamburgers, six vote for tacos, and four vote for fried chicken. Make a bar graph to organize the results of the poll.

Right away the question made me think about Dulcie's dog, Taco. Which made me think about Dulcie. Which made me think about Trish. And LaMar. And Zack. Except for LaMar, every single one of them was mad at me! The thought shocked me so much I closed the book. If things kept up like this, I wasn't going to have a single friend left. And it wasn't even my fault. *They* were the ones picking on *me*!

9

Grrrrrrrr!

Friday night after practice I hurried home to get Muggsy ready for the dog show. He needed a bath and a blow-dry with Mom's hair dryer. And I needed to wolf down some dinner.

I put Muggsy into the bathtub and went to work while Mom cooked me a couple of hot dogs and some frozen fries. It would have been better if she'd left out the side of green beans, but she's got this thing about vegetables. She thinks they're as important as basketball.

"Look, Mickey, I made something for Muggsy," she said after I managed to force down a few beans. "I thought he ought to look nice for the show." She held up a big fluffy green and white bow with a little plastic basketball glued to the center.

"Wow! Thanks, Mom! That's so cool!" I said. It *was* cool too. But I knew it was going to take more than a flashy bow to make the judges choose a dog who couldn't even walk in a straight line.

It was probably stupid to even enter Muggsy in

the contest. Sam Sherman was entering his black Lab, Zorro. I'd heard him talking about it earlier in the locker room. Trish was entering Gabrielle and Dulcie was entering Taco. Hundreds of kids were probably entering their dogs. Muggsy didn't have a chance. But at least people would see that he wasn't the little runt he used to be. That thought cheered me up so much I whistled as I tied Muggsy's bow to his collar. If you happen to like "Yankee Doodle," I'm a pretty good whistler.

The dog show was held at the fairgrounds. After Mom parked the car, she, Meggie, and I entered the huge building. On Sundays they have antique shows there and use all three rooms. But tonight they had closed off the third one and made one big space out of the other two.

We checked in at the desk and received our number. I wished we could have had 11, my basketball number, but it was already taken. We got 52. I attached one card with "52" to Muggsy's collar and tied the other one around the button of my shirt.

"Wow, Mickey, look at all the dogs!" Meggie exclaimed. "That one over there is sooooo bee-yoo-tee-ful!" She pointed to a sleek Irish setter being led by a kid with hair the same color as his dog's red coat.

"There's Dulcie and her mom," Mom said as

she scanned the crowd. "Linda! Hi! We're over here!" she called to Mrs. Steffins.

"MICK-EEEEEY!" Dulcie screeched. She raced around a clutch of kids and dogs to get to us. The first thing I noticed was that Taco wasn't pink anymore.

"Hey, Dulcie," I said. "Taco's looking good. How did you get the tomato juice out?"

Dulcie giggled. "We took him to the doggie beauty parlor and they made him all pretty. He even has a little scarf and a hat to wear. She reached into the pink plastic bag slung over her shoulder and pulled out a red bandana and a tiny Mexican sombrero. "Aren't these cute? And smell him!"

The last thing I wanted to do was smell Dulcie's dumb dog, but she didn't give me a choice. She picked him up and stuck him in my face. "GOOD, HUH?"

The dog smelled like Trish Riley when she sprays on too much of her mother's perfume. Yeeeeech!!

"Hi, Mickey!" Trish hollered just then. She came rushing over to us with Gabrielle. Muggsy's poor sister had the top of her hair done up in a silly doggie ponytail tied with a blue ribbon that matched the ribbons on Trish's ponytails. I felt sorry for her. No dog deserved to look that goofy.

"Hi, Trish," I greeted her. "Hey, you don't happen to know what the dogs have to do in the show, do you?"

Trish shook her head. "No, Mickey, but don't worry. They probably don't have to sit or anything."

I wasn't sure if she was trying to be nice, or reminding me that she was still sort of mad at me. I let it go.

"Attention, please!" came a voice over the loudspeaker. "Will all contestants please report to the arena? We're about to begin! All contestants to the arena, please!"

"This is it!" Trish squealed.

Mrs. Steffins tied the bandana around Taco's neck, slipped the little sombrero on his head, and tightened it with the cord. Then Dulcie, Trish, and I headed over to the arena with our dogs. Muggsy strained so hard at his leash it took everything I had to hold him in line.

A dumb song about doggies in the window blared through the big room. There were 73 people and 73 dogs in the parade. Slowly, we all moved around the ring in front of the judges' table.

One of the judges was the guy who owns the pet shop on Wooster Street. Another was Dr. Barry, the vet who'd saved Muggsy's life. I started to grin at her, but thought it might be cheating, and caught myself just in time.

Muggsy pranced along happily. I could feel myself relaxing as we rounded the bend at the starting point for the second time. After we made the twelfth loop, everybody cleared the ring and waited for the judges to make their choices. The original 73 dogs would be narrowed down to 20. I knew Muggsy and I didn't have a chance, but it still felt like we had to wait forever. Finally, the announcer's voice boomed over the loudspeaker again.

"Will numbers 41, 13, 67, 52, 2, ..."

"Mickey! That's you! They said your number!" Trish squealed in my ear. Muggsy made the first cut!" She grabbed my arm and jumped up and down.

I couldn't believe it. I stood there dazed as they read the other numbers. Dulcie and Taco made it too. Trish and Gabrielle didn't. Neither did Sam Sherman and Zorro.

"This is so bogus!" Sam shouted.

We turned and looked over at him. So did just about everybody else near us. He was standing with Zorro and one of his buddies from school, waving his arms and shouting at nobody. His face was as red as Zorro's collar.

"No REAL show would choose a mutt over a

thoroughbred! At an AKC show you *run* around in the ring with your dog. You don't shuffle. And you certainly don't have 73 people and 73 dogs crammed in there all at once. I'm getting out of here!" He stomped to the exit without even looking at us.

"Someone's not happy tonight," Trish said with a grin. If she were disappointed about Gabrielle not making the cut, she didn't act like it.

Dulcie and I headed back into the ring with our dogs.

"Just relax and have fun," I told her. "It's not a big deal if you don't win. It's good to even get this far."

Dulcie rolled her eyes at me. "I KNOW that already," she answered. "I'm not stupid, Mister."

The kid in front of me snickered. Before my face turned redder than his Irish setter, a sudden blast of music brought us back to business. I tightened my grip on Muggsy's leash and entered the ring in front of Dulcie. This time I didn't know the song they were playing and didn't care. I could barely hear it over the thundering of my heart.

A smaller number of entrants meant that there were wider spaces between each of the kids and their dogs. With fewer dogs to choose from, the judges could see everyone much better—which meant that Muggsy had to be on his best behavior.

Around the ring we all paraded. Once. Twice. Three times. And each time Muggsy walked along with his head up, alert, and interested in what was going on. He was doing great. I was the one who was wasn't doing so hot. I was so nervous my hands were gushing sweat like geysers.

Five more times we made the loop. Then we left the ring to begin the long wait for the judges' decision. This time the 20 dogs would be whittled down to the final five.

I felt like a miracle had happened. I'd landed a surprise shot at the win! And now I wanted it so bad the wanting seeped out of my skin and formed a cloud around me. Dulcie and Trish were next to me chattering, but I couldn't see or hear them from the center of the cloud.

Finally, when it seemed as if I couldn't wait one more second, the announcement came. "May I have your attention, please?" the loudspeaker voice boomed. "The judges's decision is in. The final five are: number 36, Mallory Jenkins with Angel; number 2, Eric Mathews with Lucky; number 49, Dulcie Ann Steffins with Taco, ..."

"Oh, that's so GOOD!" Dulcie hollered. The grown-ups around us smiled.

I tensed my muscles and waited.

" ... number 16, Alex Cline with J.J., and ..."

I squeezed my eyes shut and prayed hard.

" ... and number 27, Michael Mendelssohn with Maxine."

I opened my eyes and looked around, dazed. Muggsy hadn't won. And now he was barking at a poodle. Mom came over and took him from me. "You guys did so well," she said. "I'm so proud of you, honey."

"Let's get out of here," I mumbled heading for the door.

"Mickey!" Mom grabbed my sleeve and yanked me back. "We can't leave now when Dulcie and Taco are still in the contest."

I didn't say anything. Trish had moved closer to the ring to get a better view. I just stayed where I was and tried not to let anybody see the war going on inside me. It was so unfair.

What did Dulcie do to deserve to make it to the top five? She hadn't worked nearly as hard as I had. She hadn't tried to train Taco. And she sure hadn't helped me train Muggsy. All she'd done was eat my last slice of baloney.

The announcer's voice sliced into my angry thoughts. "Ladies and gentlemen, this is our final round. Here the judges are going to be looking not only at the health, friendliness, and overall attractiveness of the dogs, but also at how well they can control themselves. The contestants will now be asked to walk around the arena one at a time. At the cue they will be asked to command their dog to sit."

After that I never heard another word. My heart was pounding with a weird kind of excitement. No way could Dulcie get Taco to sit. He wasn't as wild as Muggsy, but he wouldn't win any gold stars for obedience either. A mean little part of me felt happy enough to do somersaults. If a nice, big, happy-looking dog like Muggsy couldn't win, then a short, skinny, hairless one didn't deserve to win either.

I moved closer to the arena to watch. The first kid, Mallory whatever-her-name-was, did great. The second kid, the one with the Irish setter that matched his hair, did well too. And then it was Dulcie's turn. She walked out and grinned at the audience. She and Taco were practically prancing. At the cue from the judge, they stopped.

"SIT, TACO!" Dulcie yelled. "SIT!"

Taco sat. Both front paws hit the ground. He looked up at Dulcie and cocked his head in his little sombrero—and stayed until Dulcie yelled, "GOOD, TACO! NOW WALK WITH ME!"

My eyes popped in disbelief. They were still the size of snowballs when Dulcie skipped out of the ring.

"How did you do that?" I demanded when she rejoined us. "Taco couldn't do that before."

Dulcie grinned. "I did the clicker thing like you were trying to do with Muggsy," she said. "Only I think I did it better, Mickey."

I pretended to be busy watching the last two contestants. Suddenly it seemed too hot in the building. I grabbed the neck of my shirt and fanned it in and out. What did she mean she did it better? *I* was the one who taught *her* how to do it in the first place!

After what seemed like two years, the announcer's voice came back one last time. "What a hard choice this has been!" he shouted. "But the judges have finally reached their decision."

"Can we go now?" I asked Mom.

"Shhhhhhhh," she whispered. She was holding one of Dulcie's hands and Mrs. Steffins was holding the other. They were all three giggling and looking at each other.

"The winner of the first citywide dog show is ..." he said, pausing for effect, "Dulcie Ann Steffins and Taco!"

Thunderous applause broke out around the big room. Mom and Mrs. Steffins both hugged Dulcie who tossed her fuzzy hair and led her dog back to the arena to claim their prize. If she smiled any wider, her face would have cracked. I stared in disbelief.

All of a sudden I understood Trish Riley a whole lot better. She wasn't the only one who was jealous of a four-year-old and a skinny, hairless dog!

10

A Long Walk Home

Marcus Bennett lunged in front of me. I pivoted right. Left. Left again. By the time he figured out he'd been zapped by the Spider Strategy, I was on a collision course with the basket. I tore down the court like a man being chased—which is exactly what I was. A gang of Pirates thundered at my heels, ready to have me for lunch.

I was almost there—so close that the tips of my fingers could feel the ball drop through the hoop. And then—from out of nowhere—Marcus Bennett copped a steal and whipped in a layup. I hadn't seen him coming.

"Move, Shrimpo! MOVE!" Sam Sherman yelled behind me.

I moved. Down the court I roared to the Seville Pirates' basket. But I ran like a blind guy. I was still so dazzled by Bennett's quick move, I could barely take in what was happening.

It was the morning after the dog show and I was still smarting from Dulcie's win. But even so, I was putting everything I had into this game—

which was more than you could say for Zack. If such a thing were possible, he was playing even worse than he had during practice.

At halftime Coach jumped all over him.

"Zeno, you in this game or not?" he demanded. "Because if you're not, you're off the floor. You have exactly five minutes to show me what you can do. In case you've forgotten, this is the big one. B-I-G O-N-E!"

I glanced over at Zack, glad Coach was chewing him out. It was about time! Zack stared at the floor, a muscle twitching in his cheek. I didn't feel one bit sorry for him. I'd been trying to tell him for the past two weeks to get the lead out, but he never listened. And now we were going to lose and it was going to be all his fault. Well, maybe not *all* his fault. But a lot his fault.

I went for my water bottle. When I came back Zack was nowhere in sight. "Where's Zack?" I asked Nick Clemmons. I didn't really care where he was. Yet an uneasy feeling nagged at me like a toothache.

Nick shrugged. "I don't know. Out back, I think," he said.

I sat on the bench and took a swig of water. The uneasy feeling grew. I tried stuffing it down, but it kept growing like one of those giant weeds that spring up overnight.

I had no choice. I had to get up and head for the door that opened off the locker room. It led outside to a concrete pad where the trash bin was. The least I could do was drag Zack back into the locker room so he wouldn't be late. Halftime shows don't last forever.

I wasn't planning to say anything to him except, "Get back inside." That's it. If I said anything else I'd blow like a volcano. I wasn't doing it for him anyway. I was doing it for the team.

A slap of cold air greeted me as I pulled open the door. Goose bumps dotted my bare legs and arms, but I stepped outside and looked around. No Zack. I started to turn around when I spotted a flash of green on the side of the Dumpster.

"Zack? You out here?" I called. I was unwilling to go any closer in case the door locked behind me.

No answer.

"Hey, guys!" I called inside. "If this locks, open it for me, okay?"

"Sure!" Tony Anzaldi hollered back. "Where are you going?"

I knew Coach would have a fit if he saw me going outside now, so I didn't answer. I carefully closed the door behind me and ran over to where I'd seen the flash of green. Zack wasn't there. I headed around the other side of the Dumpster just as he was turning the corner in front of it. The chase made me mad enough to pop. I wasn't out here to play "Ring-around-the Rosy"!

"Just knock it off, Zack!" I growled. "It's bad enough that ..."

Zack turned to look at me. Tears were raining down his face. Tears just like the day his Dad left for Minnesota. The sight of them stopped me cold.

"Zack? What's wrong? Are you crying over what Coach said?" I couldn't believe that was it. Zack's no wimp. If he was crying, there must be something worth crying about.

"What do you care?" he snarled. "You're BUSY, remember?"

I'd started to say something, but that shut me up. Suddenly I felt confused—like something really big was going on and I didn't understand it.

"I'm scared, Mick," Zack blurted. "I'm really, really scared! Ever since we got close to the play-off game it's like I ... I ..." He stopped and wiped his eyes with the back of his hand. "Oh, man, this is stupid trying to talk to you. You don't care!"

That wasn't true. I did care. I cared more than I even knew I did. Zack was my best friend. And he was hurting bad. He'd tried to tell me, but I'd been too into my own stuff to notice. All the times he'd given me a hint flashed in front of me at once.

"Listen, Zack," I said. "I know you've been trying to tell me all along, but I couldn't hear you. Well, now I can! I hear you Zack, I hear you!"

Zack choked back a sob.

"Listen to me," I pleaded. "You can do this! You *can*! WE can! We work together like—like ..." I groped for something to compare us to. "Like a car and an engine," I said finally. It was lame, but it was the best I could do.

"Please, Zack!" I pleaded when he still didn't answer. "Do you remember my friend Tom at Meadowview?" Tom "Stringbean" Jackson is this old-time basketball star I'd met at Christmas when we'd taken our dogs to the nursing home. I hadn't seen him in a while, but something he once told me offered itself like a gift to Zack.

"Tom told me that we can do all things in God," I said. "Not just some things, Zack. But *all* things. And that means hard things. *Really* hard things that scare your socks off. All we have to do is trust in Him."

Zack swallowed hard.

"It's true! Just try it and see if it isn't!" I begged. "Now come back in with me. We'll work together. I'll help you and you can help me. We'll pretend like we're at some old game that doesn't even count. Okay?"

For a long time Zack stood next to the big

Dumpster scrubbing his face with the hem of his shirt. Then, without a word, he moved toward the door. I held my breath hoping it wasn't locked. I'd sure hate to have to pound on the door and have Coach find out we'd left the building. But the door opened and we went back in. The blast of warm, steamy air from the locker room made me shiver. I'd forgotten how cold it was outside.

The second half of the final game began with a ball of fire rolling down center court. Sam Sherman came on in a blaze. Point by point he raised our score until we were neck-and-neck with the Pirates. They scored. We scored. They scored. We scored. On and on it went, point for point. The crowd was wired.

"SAM! SAM! HE'S OUR MAN! IF HE CAN'T DO IT, NO ONE CAN!" the cheerleaders screamed.

Usually that's my least favorite cheer. Unless, of course, they're saying it for me. But today I didn't care. I kept my eye on Zack. Little by little, he loosened up.

The clock was running down when suddenly I got the ball for the first time in the second half. It came hard and fast from Sam Sherman. I went to pass and couldn't. A Pirate jumped in front of me, waving his arms like a madman. I pivoted right. Left. And left again. No good! He knew the

Spider Strategy and it wasn't going to work this time.

"Mick!"

A voice beside me spun me to the left a third time. Zack stood like a tower of sand bags, ready to hold back the flood. His feet clamped the floor. One hand gripped the other in a low, steady fist. He'd set me a pick—right when I needed it!

I moved out away from him, then zipped in close. So close that not even a skinny little Pirate would have fit between me and my best buddy. This was my moment to fake them out. Coach had said to change the pace or run in the opposite direction. Only there wasn't time to do either one. With one second left on the clock, there was only one thing to do. Make it or break it.

I said a quick prayer and shot from the three-point zone.

Zoom! Straight into the basket it soared, as smooth as whipped cream.

The noise from the stands bounced off the walls. The team stood there, dazed, just staring at each other. We'd done it! Somehow we'd claimed the championship! The huge trophy was ours!

Pinecrest fans stormed the court. Suddenly I was up in the air, held up by the arms of the cheering crowd. I looked over at Sam Sherman and he was up in the air too. I scanned the mob still in the stands cheering, trying to find my parents.

"OVER HERE, MICKEY!" A voice yelled. It was faint in the rumble of shouts, but I heard it. A skinny little girl with the wildest hair that ever grew out of a human head was in the front row jumping up and down waving a sign. Even though it was upside-down, but I had no trouble reading it. It said:

Me for Mickey.

I'm not kidding—it was almost my turn to cry. I'd been so worried about myself and all that junk I had to do, I'd forgotten what really counted. Zack, Trish, LaMar, even the noisy little kid who's "only this many." My *friends*.

As soon as my feet hit the ground, Trish rushed over with Ken. "Mickey!" she screeched. "Ken got some great shots for our video! He got you making the winning three-pointer!"

I looked from Trish, to Ken, my head reeling. "Huh? The v-v-video's not done?" I stammered. "You mean you didn't make it without me?"

Trish laughed. "Of course not, Mickey. It's *your* video. And this afternoon we're going to do the part with you and Muggsy, okay?"

"O-o-kay," I stuttered. I felt like the wind had been knocked out of me.

I looked around for Zack and found him in the throng of people. I had to elbow my way through to get to him. "We did it, buddy!" I shouted, pounding him on the back. "We did it! Didn't I tell you we could?"

Zack pounded me back. It was all the answer I needed. We were still friends. I'd sort of forgotten about God too in all this pressure. But God definitely hadn't forgotten about me! "You're one lucky guy, Mickey McGhee," I told myself as I waved to the crowd.

"Mickey, honey!" It was my mom. Normally I don't go in for mushy stuff in front of the guys, but today I didn't care. I even let her kiss me in public. She kissed Zack too.

"I'm making you guys the biggest, cheesiest pizza on the planet," she said. "Let's get Dad and Meggie and go home. We've got celebrating to do! I'll even make a chocolate cake for dinner tonight!"

Zack nodded eagerly.

"You guys go ahead," I said. "I want to walk, okay? I'll catch up with you at home."

I figured everybody would protest. Or that Zack would offer to walk home with me. Or Meggie would beg and plead until Mom let her walk too. But nobody said anything except, "All right. But hurry, okay?"

"Sure," I said, meaning it. There's nothing I like better than pizza with the works and my mom's Texas sheet cake. But there was plenty of time for those things. But first I needed to have a lo-o-o-o-o-o-o-ng talk with Somebody else I'd been ignoring—God! There's no better time for it than on a long walk home.

```
F Kin
Kindig, Tess Eileen.
   March mainia
```